THE TEAM
WITH THE
GHOST
PLAYER

" They played the video again, all staring
at the screen.

There was no player near Jacky. But, just
for a split second, Alex had seen a boot with a
red sock above it. A disembodied leg and a
boot, studs up, smashing into the back of
Jacky's knee.

Ridiculous. But she'd seen it. And so, she
was sure, had some of the others. "

More great reads in the SHADES 2.0 series:

THE TEAM
WITH THE
GHOST
PLAYER

Dennis Hamley

Ransom

SHADES 2.0

The Team with the Ghost Player

by Dennis Hamley

Published by Ransom Publishing Ltd.

Radley House, 8 St. Cross Road, Winchester, Hampshire SO23 9HX, UK

www.ransom.co.uk

ISBN   978 178127 637 2

First published in 2014

ONE

Leabharlanna Fhine Gall

The chairman's office in the main stand always seemed dark and gloomy. Team photographs hung from the wood-panelled walls. Big men with big boots, brawny folded arms and baggy shorts glared balefully out of black and white prints. SEASON 1912-1913, 1920-21, 1931-32, 1938-39.

Three men were in the office. The chairman,

fat and red-faced, sat at his huge desk. Another man in his fifties stood behind him.

The chairman put his half-chewed cigar down on an ashtray and looked at the third man. Big, burly and strong as this man was, and though he could probably squash the chairman with one blow of his fist, he stood fearfully in front of the desk.

'You're finished here,' said the chairman. 'And I'll make sure you never play football again, not First Division, not Third, not even a village team.'

The big man shifted from foot to foot, but said nothing.

'You're lucky,' said the chairman. 'By rights I should get the police here. You deserve five years inside for what you did.'

The big man looked at the floor.

'But I won't have this great club mired in scandal. We'll keep it to ourselves. Just get out of my sight and never come back.'

The third man spoke. The club manager. 'Best do as he says, Wilf,' he said.

The big man spoke at last. 'You could have spoken up for me. But you didn't.'

'It's over,' said the manager. 'Best go now.'

'But what will I do?' said the big man.

'There's a war coming,' said the chairman. 'Join the Army. Best place for you. Now get out.'

Trembling with suppressed anger, the big man left the room, stamped downstairs and out into the dusky evening.

He turned, looked back at the stands and terraces, silhouetted against the darkening sky, threw back his head and shouted deep-felt words:

'I curse this club. May it go down to the depths and never come back. I curse the chairman, the board, the manager. I curse every player who will ever turn out for it. Especially the scrawny young ones who try to fill the boots of their elders and betters. May they all rot in hell.'

Then he turned on his heel and walked bitterly along the street. A newspaper placard caught his eye.

HITLER INVADES POLAND

He made up his mind and headed straight for the Army recruiting office. Nine months later, he was killed at Dunkirk.

A packed Harbour Park, home of Greyport FC. League One. Greyport versus MK Dons. Greyport leading 1-0.

If they can get three points today then they're in the automatic promotion places. Fifteen minutes to go and just six weeks before the end of the season.

Jacky Warren is playing his first game for Greyport. He's seventeen and has come through the Academy, the youth team and the reserves. And now, months before he expected it, here he is playing with the seniors.

He isn't overawed. He knows he's good. He looks across at Bart Samuels, thirty-seven and never played higher than League One. That won't do for Jacky. He has it all worked out. Premiership by twenty, in Europe the year after, World Cup when he's twenty-two.

Dmitri Sverdlov pushes the ball out to him. He controls it neatly and looks round. He's in space. The Dons defence retreats. He will run with the ball and then slip it to Ronnie Hughes on the wing, who'll work it down the right and cross neatly onto the head of Lee Benson, striker, and then they'll be two-up.

It will be the perfect goal.

So what's this red shadow crowding him from the left? What's this searing pain, this crushing blow on the back of his knee? Is his cruciate ligament snapped? Whose malignant voice hisses, '*Hold that one, you little runt?*' so savagely?

He's down on the grass in agony. The referee stops play. Bill Oates, the trainer, runs out. He stoops and feels Jacky's knee. Jacky yells with pain.

'Can you stand up?'

No, he can't.

Bill signals for the stretcher. A substitute peels off his tracksuit and runs on to the pitch.

The home dressing room was empty except

for Bill and Jacky.

'What happened?' asked Bill.

Jacky had been given a numbing injection. The pain was less. Anger replaced it.

'It was a filthy foul,' he shouted. 'Why wasn't the rat sent off?'

There was silence.

'Who do you mean?' said Bill. 'There was nobody near you. You just collapsed on the ground.'

He had taken Jacky's boot off and peeled off his sock. 'Funny,' he said. 'Your socks are mangled and there are stud marks on the back of your leg.' He touched it gingerly and Jacky winced. 'I reckon you might have done some damage there,' he said.

'It was this huge bloke.' Jacky was nearly screaming. 'He steamed up on my left. Wearing red. It was deliberate. Studs up.

He meant to hurt.'

'Jacky,' said Bill. 'Trust me, there was nobody there. And besides, MK Dons don't play in red. *We* do.'

Jock Mackenzie, the Greyport manager, came into the dressing room. Jacky had huge respect for him. Eighty caps for Scotland, played for Celtic, Liverpool and Juventus, one of the football greats.

He looked down at Jacky, his face serious.

'Get yourself well, laddie,' he said. 'I need you.' The noise of the crowd carried down into the dressing room. As Bill looked at Jacky's leg, a loud collective groan sounded down the tunnel.

'I'm needed up there as well,' said Jock, and left quickly.

'It sounds like the Dons have equalised,'

said Bill. 'But it was good of the gaffer to come down and say that to you.'

The paramedics arrived and cleaned out the bleeding stud marks. Then the club doctor examined him and phoned the hospital. The club physio manipulated Jacky's leg, making him roar with pain again. The roar got mixed up with the crowd's frenzy outside and both died away in another monstrous groan.

'Listen to them,' said Bill. 'We've lost.'

'They'll blame me,' said Jacky.

'No they won't,' said Bill.

But they did.

TWO

Jacky didn't like being in hospital. He hated ice baths and then having his leg suspended in the air. When he asked why, the nurse just said, 'When the head is pale, lift the tail,' and carried on with what she was doing. There was real hurt despite the painkillers. He endured tests, X-rays, a nearly sleepless night and then a doctor

Leabharlanna Fhine Gall

looking down on him and saying, 'We think you've done something serious to your cruciate ligament. You won't be playing again for six months.'

'If ever,' Jacky muttered.

'I didn't say that,' said the doctor, as he walked out of the room.

Alex, his girlfriend, came round next day. She saw his pain-filled face.

He seized her hand, said, 'Am I glad to see you?' and tried a welcoming smile which failed. She hated seeing him, so bright, smart and always happy, in such depression. She bent down and kissed him.

'Everything will be all right,' she whispered. *What a pathetic thing to say*, she thought.

'No it won't,' said Jacky. 'The doc said six months. But I saw his face. He thinks I might never play again.'

She squeezed his hand. 'Yes you will,' she said. 'You're tough.'

'And nobody believes me,' he went on. 'They say I made it up and nobody touched me. Why do they say that?'

There was a commotion outside. A woman's voice shouted, 'Only two at a time.' But the door swung open and six men burst in. Greyport players.

'We've got proof that you faked it,' said Lee Benson. 'Let's see what you've got to say about this.' He waved an iPad. 'A video of the match. I paused it in the right place.'

The screen burst into colour. There was Jacky receiving the ball from Dmitri and moving off down the pitch. Alex thought how graceful he looked. Anyone could see what a quality player he was. She saw how, without slackening speed, he looked round, judging the play. She knew he had picked

Ronnie out and would pass to him.

And then, suddenly, he stopped. She saw his head and shoulders arch backwards. She saw pain and shock together in his face. And then he was on the ground, rolling and screaming in agony.

'Doesn't that prove it?' said Bart Samuels. 'You were shamming. There was no one near you. You should have been sent off.'

You can talk, thought Alex. *I've heard people say you're the worst diver in the league.*

'We lost because of you,' said Ronnie. 'We couldn't get going again. That was our big chance to go top. We'll be stuck in this league for ever.'

'But I … ' started Jacky. Then he fell back on the pillows. 'Oh, what's the point of talking to you lot? You've made up your minds and nothing will change them.'

But something wasn't right.

'Just a minute,' said Alex. 'Play it again.'

'It won't be any different,' said Lee. 'Replays always come out the same, however much you wish they wouldn't.' But he showed it again nevertheless.

Alex watched, very carefully. Then she said, 'Now! Pause it.'

The picture froze.

'There's something there,' she said. 'Go back again.'

'Anything to please a lady,' said Bart sarcastically.

Once again the picture came to life.

'Stop,' cried Alex. 'Look.'

They looked.

'What is it?' said Dmitri.

'Nothing,' said Bart.

'Yes there is,' said Alex. 'I see a boot. A big, old-fashioned boot.'

Lee played it yet again. They all stared at the screen.

There was no player near Jacky. But, just for a split second, Alex had seen a boot with a red sock above it. A disembodied leg and a boot, studs up, smashing into the back of Jacky's knee.

Ridiculous. But she'd seen it. And so, she was sure, had some of the others.

'It is leg,' said Dmitri.

Not everyone agreed. 'This is crazy,' said Bart. 'It's just a trick of the light.'

'Well, I think there's something weird going on,' said Ronnie.

'What, a ghost boot?' Bart laughed derisively. 'When you've been in this game as long as I have, you'll see things a bit differently.'

'What's that supposed to mean?' said Ronnie.

'What I say,' said Bart. 'If you're hurt, that's part of the game; you just have to take it. If you fake it, you should be kicked out.'

Jacky put his head in his hands. 'Oh, what's the use of trying to tell you lot what happened?' he said.

'What *did* happen?' said Lee.

'I saw him,' said Jacky. 'I knew he was behind me. Then I felt this terrible blow to the back of my knee. I can't describe the pain.' His face creased up with the memory, as if it was happening again. 'When I opened my eyes, there he was.'

'Who was?' said Ronnie.

'The player who fouled me. He looked down as if he was satisfied, as if he'd done his job well. And he said, "There, now you've gone the way of all the others." '

Alex spoke. 'What was he like, Jacky?'

'Great barrel chest. Big jowly face. Black shiny hair, as if he put grease on it. He looked like he could pick me up and break me in half if he wanted to. He had a really old shirt on. All red, but no logo, no sponsor name. It had a collar and buttons. Baggy white shorts. Red and white socks. Big leather boots with huge toecaps.'

'Sounds like Greyport before you were born,' said Bart. 'Has someone been showing you old photos?'

'You're making it up,' said Wally.

Jacky slumped back onto his pillow. 'No I'm not,' he said despairingly. 'It sounds crazy, but it's true.'

'What did he mean by, "You've gone the way of all the others?"' said Alex.

Before Jacky could answer, Bart said, 'I'm fed up with this. If you're going on with that rubbish then I'm out of here. Have a nice evening with your girlfriend.'

He turned on his heel and walked out of the ward.

There was a strange expression on Bart's face which Alex couldn't understand. The others looked at each other. Then Lee said, 'I'm off too.' He didn't sound happy.

The others followed. Alex watched them. *Why are they following Bart? They don't have to. And I don't think they want to, either.'*

Jacky's eyes were shut. Alex thought he was asleep. But when they were alone, he opened them.

'Except for Bart, I think they believe me,' he said. 'But they're as scared as I am.'

'Why scared?' asked Alex. 'Curious, yes. Worried too, but not scared, surely?'

'You didn't see him,' said Jacky, so quietly that Alex had to bend down to hear him.

'He was *evil*. He wanted me *dead*. I know he did. If I can't play again, I'm as good as. That's why I'm scared.

'He's in my dreams now. There's triumph in his eyes. He could break me in half with those arms. He could cripple me for life with those boots.' He winced. 'I think he has.'

Alex didn't answer. If she tried, she knew she'd cry.

'The painkillers make me drowsy,' said Jacky. 'I have to sleep now. I don't want to, because I'll see him again. But I can't help it. Goodbye, love.'

His eyes closed again. Alex watched him for a few minutes. Then, when she was sure he was asleep, she quietly left.

THREE

The nightmare came quickly. Jacky stood alone in suffocating darkness like black cotton wool. He knew he was waiting for something.

As he stood wondering, it seemed as though the cotton wool sky lightened slightly and hard-edged shapes were silhouetted against it, somehow threatening. He looked at them, mystified. He knew he'd seen them before in a place he knew very well. But where?

He felt deep down that something was approaching and that it was dangerous, evil.

Suddenly he knew where he was. Outside Harbour Park. The shapes were the roofs of the stands, leaning over the terracing like the long heads of dinosaurs. 'Here he comes,' they seemed to say in echoing, metallic voices. 'You can't stop him.'

And there he was. Huge, immeasurably strong, mightily powerful. Red shirt, big boots, baleful expression.

He spoke. His cavernous voice reverberated inside Jacky's head. 'You're just one of many. How do you like being finished before you start?'

In his dream, Jacky was paralysed with fear.

The creature threw his head back and seemed to shout at the sky. Terrible words of profound, brain-rending rage were pouring out of his mouth.

But Jacky only saw a mouth working silently and heard none of them. The silence made the terror lift a little and he slipped easily into a deep and dreamless sleep.

Alex couldn't sleep. Her mind was churning with strange thoughts about this extraordinary day.

First, the video. She was almost glad that Jacky had talked about a ghostly figure. The idea of a disembodied leg on a TV screen wasn't only a bit frightening, but also completely daft. If she told anyone who wasn't there, they'd laugh.

Who'd believe that a TV camera could catch a tiny bit of the supernatural?

But now it wasn't just a paranormal leg but a whole body. She saw it in her mind's eye just as Jacky described it, and she knew he was telling the truth. She knew about footballers diving and pretending to be injured. Bart was right in one thing.

'If you fake it, you should be kicked out.'

But this wasn't a dive. It was real. And it made her want to cry. Her Jacky, cut down when his longed-for life in football had hardly started. Why? Why should it happen to this lovely man she cared for so much and who didn't have a vengeful bone in his body?

She remembered how her friends had reacted when she told them she was going out with a footballer.

'*You want to watch them. They're plastered all over 'Hello' and 'OK'.*'

'*Will you be one of the WAGs then?*'

'*Are you after his two hundred grand a week?*'

She couldn't be bothered to tell them

that, far from two hundred grand a week, at his age Jacky hardly got two hundred. Anyway, she didn't want to be one of the WAGs and he would not, definitely *not*, ever be in *Hello* and *OK*. Not if she could help it, anyway.

Suddenly, she had a dreadful thought. The figure had said, '*You've gone the way of all the others.*'

What did that mean? Had something like this happened before?

Before she could answer her own question, she fell asleep. But not before she had resolved to find out.

She woke next morning with two possibilities. The first was the public library. The second was her Uncle Stanley. The library was obvious. She could find books and read old newspapers. Uncle Stanley might be even better. He'd supported Greyport all his life and there was nothing he didn't know about them. Or so he claimed.

The prospect didn't exactly thrill her. She wasn't really interested in football, except for one person who played it. But she had to do it. For his sake.

The library was quiet. She had no intention of borrowing a book and taking it home. She would do her reading there, surrounded by students with laptops.

She found a likely book on the sports shelves, *Pride of the City: a History of Greyport FC*, and looked through it. There were lists of players and lots of league tables, but not much history that she could see. Her heart sank.

But she kept on reading and soon found

out something she'd never realised. Before the war, in the 20s and 30s, Greyport were a big club, in the First Division with the likes of Manchester United and Arsenal. They won the league three times and the FA Cup twice.

But after 1946, when football started again after the war, they dropped down the divisions, Second, Third, Fourth, once nearly out of the Football League altogether.

When the Premiership started in 1993, they were in the old Fourth Division. Where they were now was the highest they'd been for years.

Why should that be? Was it important?

She looked closer. Greyport were relegated to the Second Division in the first season after the war, and into Division Three North the season after. And there they stayed for eight years.

Then, in 1954, they went back into the Second, what they call the Championship now. In 1956 they were nearly promoted to the First. But they slumped at the end of the season and missed out.

The next year they were relegated again and back in the Third for another eight years.

Alex didn't need to read any more. The pattern was clear.

Greyport kept trying to pick themselves up. Every time they looked as if they might, they slipped back and stayed there for years. And then they tried to rise again. And failed. Every ten or so years. Almost as if it were a timetable.

This was strange. But did it matter? Was it happening again? When was the last time they were nearly promoted?

She looked at the league tables. In 2002 they were promoted from the old Third Division to the Second. In 2004 they were top till nearly the end of the season. Then they went to pieces, lost six games in a row and finished seventh. It was a recurring pattern.

Was it just coincidence?

She turned back to the part of the book which told the club's story and looked for the 2003-04 season.

It was all about great victories, stunning goals and the special exploits of one player. Jimmy Cross. He was eighteen. He came into the team a month into the season and was brilliant straight away. Though young, he made the team tick. A great career lay in front of him.

Then, in a match away to Crewe Alexandra, when Greyport were 1-0 up with five minutes to go, he suddenly crumpled to the ground. It must have been because of the pitch. There was nobody near him and no other reason to fall so awkwardly. He'd certainly done himself a horrific injury, because he never played again. And Greyport, for that season anyway, were finished.

Alex closed the book.

Strange thoughts were chasing round her mind. *'You'll go the way of all the others.'*

If she looked, she knew she'd find the same thing every time things were looking up for Greyport: a young player strangely injured.

It was time to see Uncle Stan.

FOUR

On her way to Uncle Stan's she called in at the hospital. Jacky looked asleep. But as Alex approached, he opened his eyes.

'Hello, love,' he said.

'How do you feel today?' Alex asked.

'Terrible.'

Alex said nothing.

Jacky went on, 'They say I'll have surgery

this week. They'll cut me open. But it won't do any good. I'm finished.'

'You can't say that,' said Alex.

'Yes I can. Because I *know*.'

He turned over in bed, so his face was away from her and his voice was muffled. 'I saw him again last night. He said I was one of many. He asked what it was like to be finished before I started.'

'You mustn't believe it,' said Alex. 'You've got to beat him.'

Jacky's face creased up with pain. 'Don't be daft. It hasn't happened to you.'

Alex changed the subject. 'Have you ever heard of Jimmy Cross?'

'No. Why should I?'

'Ten years ago he was injured playing for Greyport. There was nobody near him when he fell. Just like you.'

'Oh yes? Is he still playing?'

'No,' said Alex. 'He never played again.'

'Well, there you are then,' said Jacky.

He closed his eyes again. Alex wondered if she ought to leave and let him sleep. But then he opened them.

'Do you know what upsets me nearly the most?' he said.

'No. What?' said Alex.

'That goal against MK Dons that never was. I had it all worked out. I'd ping the ball out to Ronnie, he'd go down the right, take it past the defender and make him look silly, then put over a perfect cross straight to Lee.

'Lee's the best striker outside the Premiership. He'd have it in the net before you could blink. We'd have been 2-0 up and second in the league. We'd be on a roll till the end of the season. Promoted at last.

'And it would have been *my* goal. I

planned it. So simple and perfect. It won't happen now. The ugly rat who smashed me up saw to that.'

'You can still be promoted,' said Alex.

'No we can't,' said Jacky. 'Greyport played last night. Midweek match. Went down 3-0 to Bristol City. They've lost it. It's all downhill from now on.'

Alex thought of something else. 'Bart Samuels has really got it in for you,' she said. 'Why's that?'

'Oh, Bart's all right. He's the same to everybody. He's got a chip on his shoulder, that's all.'

'Why?'

'He got into the first team young, like me. Crystal Palace, I think. He was an under-21 international at nineteen. Everyone thought he'd have a great career. But it all fizzled out. He was injured a few times and was never the same again. Spent his life playing for lower league teams for peanuts.'

'What's that got to do with you?'

'He resents young ones like us. Ronnie, Lee, me. He'd love to see me kicked out for faking it, and if I can't play again he won't shed any tears.'

'That's awful,' said Alex.

'No it's not. If I get well and I'm still at Greyport when I'm thirty-seven, I'll probably think the same.'

'But you won't be,' said Alex.

'Let's wait and see. I might be unemployed.'

'I've got to go now,' said Alex.

Jacky held out his hand and she took it in hers. 'Don't mind me,' he said. 'I know I'm not much company. But I do my best.'

'Don't worry,' she said. 'I might have

found something out tomorrow.'

'Such as what?'

Alex didn't stay to tell him.

Uncle Stan lived a few miles out of the city, so Alex had to catch a bus. His wife had died a few years before, but he had married again. Alex got on well with his new wife Margie.

'Come in and have a mug of hot chocolate,' she said. 'Stanley's upstairs in his workroom. Well, that's what he calls it. It looks like the council tip to me. And it's all about that club. He could write an encyclopaedia on Greyport.'

Stan shuffled downstairs. 'Well, what is it you want to know, Alex?'

She told them the whole story. She didn't expect them to believe a word of it, but when she had finished she saw Stan was deep in thought.

There was an expectant silence. Then he said, 'This rings a very faint bell in my mind but I can't quite say what it is.'

'Do you believe what Jacky said?' Alex asked.

'I'll have to think about that,' said Stan. 'Is he sure the shirt was all red?'

'He says so,' Alex replied. 'All red with no sponsor's name on the front. It had a collar and buttons. Very old-fashioned.'

'And he's sure the collar was red?'

'I think he'd have said if it wasn't. Why do you ask?'

'When football started again after the war, Greyport had new shirts,' said Stan. 'They were still red, but with white collars and cuffs. They've kept a bit of white on every shirt they've worn since. So if he did see a player with a red collar to his shirt, he must be from 1939 or before.'

As Alex digested this information Stan was looking through a drawer. 'I've got a collection of team photographs from way back in here,' he said. He pulled out four. 'Here are the photos from 1935 to 1939. If Jacky recognises anyone in them, I might believe him.'

On the way home, Alex looked at the photographs. Strong men with stern faces stared back at her over the years. Was Jacky's scourge among them?

She ached for them to come alive so she could ask them.

FIVE

Visiting time in the hospital again. Jacky still seemed very depressed.

'More tests and X-rays today,' he said. 'I'm fed up with it. They're operating tomorrow evening. Can't come soon enough. When it's over I can think straight.'

'I've got some old team photos,' said

Alex. 'Uncle Stan wants to know if you recognise anyone in them.'

'Give them here,' said Jacky listlessly.

She handed him the photographs. He looked at the first. Season 1935-36.

Suddenly he gasped. *'There he is!'*

'Let me see,' said Alex.

Jacky's hand shook as he pointed to a man in the second row. He was big. His arms were folded. His hair was dark and thick, his expression impassive. But there was fierceness in his eyes, so strong that it made Alex shiver.

'I'd know him anywhere,' said Jacky.

'Let's look at the other photos,' said Alex.

1936-37. He was there again, this time standing furthest on the right in the back row.

1937-38. Still in the back row, but this time on the left and now staring balefully.

1938-39. Back row again. This time he was in the centre. He was by far the tallest and burliest player there. And now his face had an expression of rage and hate which took Alex's breath away.

Jacky closed his eyes. 'Take him away from me,' he moaned.

'You've got to face him,' said Alex. She looked at the name on each photograph. '*W. Shadbolt*,' she said. 'I'll ask Uncle Stan about him.'

'I don't want to know,' Jacky muttered.

'If you want to get through this, you'll have to,' Alex replied.

'I've got enough to think about. There's the operation tomorrow. I don't want a nightmare about him tonight.'

Alex saw what he meant and she didn't blame him.

As Alex was on the bus the next evening, Jacky was just going under the anaesthetic. She wished she was at the hospital waiting for him to come round. But what she might find out now could be just as important.

Uncle Stan was waiting.

'Well?' he said.

She handed back the photographs and said, 'Yes, Jacky recognised someone. W. Shadbolt. Do you know about him?'

'Wilf Shadbolt? Yes, I certainly do. Not everything, but enough to know it's a very strange story.'

'Tell me.'

'Wilfred Shadbolt played for Greyport from 1923 right through to 1939. Sixteen years with no other club. In 1939 he was thirty-seven.'

The same as Bart Samuels, Alex thought.

'People say he was the best defender

Greyport ever had. But in 1939 he was kicked out. Just like that. No reason given. That was a terrible thing to do to a man so loyal to the club. Still, footballers then got five pounds a week and no say in anything. They were slaves. Not like today.'

'That's awful,' said Alex.

'There were rumours flying round. Greyport had signed Ted Battersby, a young defender from Aston Villa. It was obvious why. Wilf couldn't go on playing forever. Someone had to take his place, and Ted was only twenty and a good centre-half.

'The rumour was that Wilf just couldn't take it, and when they were playing a five-a-side game in training, he tackled Ted so hard that he crippled him for life. It was grievous bodily harm.

'If Ted had gone to the police about it,

Wilf could have got ten years. To keep it quiet, the chairman got rid of him. Wilf joined the army, the war started and he was killed.'

'If that's true, then he hasn't stopped doing it,' said Alex. 'He's taking a long revenge on the young.'

'That's going too far,' said Stan. 'How do you know Jacky's not making this up? Perhaps he knew Wilf Shadbolt's story better than I did.'

'That's not fair,' said Alex. 'He's seen Wilf's ghost. You haven't. You don't know.'

'No, I don't,' said Stan. 'And I'll take a lot of convincing.'

'Wilf Shadbolt said, *"You'll go the way of all the others"*,' said Alex. 'I think I know how Bart Samuels feels now.'

'Bart's been a good player for us,' said Stan. 'But he's slowed up a lot. A footballer's life is short and he's nearly past being useful. The day he's playing in a big game and he's substituted by a young player on the way up when things look a bit desperate, that's when he'll know it's all finished. And you can't help feeling sorry for him.'

'So what was true for Wilf Shadbolt then is true for Bart now,' said Alex.

'Yes,' said Stan. 'Whatever he did, I can't help feeling sorry for Wilf, too.'

SIX

Alex didn't go home straight away.
Something was nagging at her brain:
something she had to deal with.

She hadn't planned to go to Harbour
Park. She suddenly felt she had to, as if
something was guiding her.

It was quite a long journey. Darkness had

fallen when she got there. The only light came from the street lamps.

She stood outside the ground, seeing the roofs of the stands brooding over the pitch like strange birds looking after their young. A few windows were lit up. Someone working late, she supposed.

She waited. Her heart was beating fast. She felt sudden fear. What of?

There was complete and chilling silence. She waited.

The street lamps dimmed. The lights in the windows went out. Time had stopped. She was standing on a tiny island surrounded by dark. And she knew something was about to happen.

Her heart pounded.

She heard footsteps behind her. She turned. There was no one there.

Then, without warning, her ears were

assailed by noise. A voice was speaking. A man's voice, loud, echoing strangely deep in her brain.

It took a few seconds to distinguish words. But when she did, she knew exactly who was speaking.

'*I curse this club. May it go down to the depths and never come back. I curse the chairman, the board, the manager. I curse every player who will ever turn out for it. Especially the scrawny young ones who try to fill the boots of their elders and betters. May they all rot in hell.*'

The voice faded. Silence again.

What had she heard? A voice from the past. A curse on the club, a threatened fate for its young players.

Now she knew what had happened. She had been taken back over the years to the expulsion of Wilfred Shadbolt.

She had heard the words. Where was the man who uttered them?

'I'm here, Miss.'

She turned. Her head swam. She nearly fainted. But she knew that she had to be strong. She forced herself to face the thing she feared.

Yes, there he was, exactly as Jacky had described. Huge, thick black hair, barrel-chested, grizzly strong, red shirt, long shorts, boots with big toecaps. Despite the darkness, the vision stood out luminously.

'Wilf?' she said tentatively.

'Yes, Miss?'

What could she say to this man? But she must speak. That was why she had been brought here.

'Why have you tried to maim the man I love?'

There, she'd said it. She knew now that

Jacky was more than just a boyfriend. She'd made a commitment. She wasn't afraid now. She would find the truth for Jacky.

Wilf's answer was simple.

'Because I said I would.'

'And Jimmy Cross?'

'The same. And all the others as well.'

'But why?'

'Because a great wrong was done to me.'

'They say you did the same thing to Ted Battersby.'

'Yes, I know they say that.'

'They say you did it because you couldn't bear to see young players coming up and taking your place.'

'*They say, they say*. Don't listen to what *they* say … '

'Well, did you?'

'No player when his playing days are nearly done wants to see his place taken.

No player wants to be not wanted any more. I was no different. But I didn't foul young Ted. I liked him. I knew he was the right one to take my place.'

'But people said you ended his career. And if you didn't, why were you kicked out?'

Wilf didn't answer for a moment.

Then he said, 'It works both ways. We don't like being pushed aside, but it's natural that the young ones want to take our place. I didn't foul Ted. I tackled him hard, just like I'd tackle anybody. He had to know what was in store for him when he played at this level. *But it wasn't a foul.*'

'So why did they say it was?'

'He went running to the chairman saying I'd tried to cripple him deliberately. That was despicable. The chairman took his side. It's what chairmen do. He'd paid a lot for

Ted and he wanted me out.

'So he got rid of me without losing a penny and his darling boy was put in my place.'

He paused.

Then he said, 'Much good it did poor Ted. The war came before the next season started and so he never got a proper chance.

'But it doesn't matter. I cursed the club and all its players, and the curse has stuck. I thought it was justice.'

'But it's not really,' said Alex. 'What has my Jacky done to deserve this?'

She couldn't quite understand the emotions which were flickering across Wilf's face. But she knew that among them were guilt – and envy.

She waited for him to speak. When at last he did, she felt a rush of tears to her eyes.

'I know it's not justice, Miss. But nobody ever said about me what you just said about him. About loving him, I mean. Never once in all my life. That's why I've come all this way to speak to you.'

'What do you want to tell me?'

'I wish that, just once, a woman had said she loved me. I would have been a better person. But I didn't think such things ever happened. Not to me, anyway. But you two … '

He paused without finishing the sentence.

Then he said, 'The curse is lifted. Your Jacky will be well again. And you've heard the last of me. I'm sorry for all the hurt I've caused. But I can rest now.'

And before her eyes he became less solid, mistier and mistier, until he was not there at all.

Alex looked at the empty space, where a visitor from beyond the grave had just spoken to her, and whispered, 'Goodbye Wilf. And thank you.'

On the way home, Alex received a text from Jacky.

Op great. CU 2moro.

SEVEN

So it wasn't the career-ending disaster everyone feared. Jacky was up in a week and back in training three weeks after that. Alex secretly wondered if Wilf had made that happen.

But it seemed he hadn't lifted the other part of the curse. Greyport went on losing. When the last day of the season came they had dropped to seventh. It was a stroke of pure luck which earned them a point in their last game, enough to put them up a place to sixth and into the play-offs.

And it was even luckier to scrape a win in the semi-final, which took them to Wembley and a chance of promotion after all.

There was a surprise when the team for Wembley was announced. Jacky was named among the substitutes.

He was thrilled but amazed. He'd done well in training, but was nowhere near match fit.

Alex had a ticket, of course. She gasped when she sat in her seat and saw the huge banking of red seats, the ground filling up, the Wembley Arch gleaming white above her and the emerald green, perfect pitch, with its white lines and goal nets rippling in the slight breeze.

Perhaps my Jacky will step onto this hallowed pitch before the day is out, she thought.

But for a long time it didn't seem possible. For most of the game Greyport were defending desperately. It was amazing that they weren't three goals down after ninety minutes. But at full time it was still nil-all.

Extra time saw no change. And still Jacky hadn't stepped out onto the green grass.

Second half of extra time. Five minutes to go. Jacky sat watching miserably. It would be a goalless draw, then penalties. And they would lose. He knew it.

He felt a hand on his shoulder. A soft Scottish voice said, 'I told you I'd need you.'

He turned and looked up. Jock Mackenzie stood there.

'I've saved you up till last,' he said. 'Get out there, boy, and show us what you're made of.'

Jacky stood up. Strength seemed to flood through him.

'Thanks, Gaffer,' he said incredulously.

He walked to the touchline. He was trembling and his heart was racing. The fourth official checked his studs and the referee beckoned him on.

Bart Samuels was called off. Jacky reached out to greet him, but Bart ran straight past without even looking at him.

Alex watched this happen, remembered what Stan had said about being substituted in a big game, and felt a wave of sorrow for both Bart and Wilf. And the other players too. They had looked at Bart and seen themselves in years to come.

Jacky was back on the pitch for the first time in six weeks. For a moment he looked round as if he'd never seen such a thing in his life. Then suddenly his mind clicked and it was as if he had never been off it.

Dmitri won the ball in the Greyport penalty area. He slipped the ball through to Jacky in midfield. Jacky took it and set off on a run. Suddenly he stopped, heart beating wildly again, waiting for the sudden crushing blow to his ankle. It never came.

But something else did. Wilf Shadbolt was standing next to him.

'I'll not bother you again,' he said. 'You'll do well. And you won't suffer like me when it's all over. You're a lucky man. You've been given a great gift. So look after that girl of yours. And *now pick it up again where you left off.'*

Then he vanished.

Now Jacky knew what he had to do. He saw Ronnie on the right and pinged the ball straight to him. He knew Ronnie would nutmeg the fullback and leave him wallowing uselessly. He knew Ronnie would cross perfectly and that Lee would rise high above the defence. He knew that Lee's bullet header would be in the net before anyone could blink.

And he was right. The perfect goal that never was. Simple but deadly. His own creation. And it had won them promotion at last. He somersaulted in joy, waved to the Greyport supporters, picked Alex out among them and blew her a kiss.

Alex, in the middle of the yelling, singing and stamping fans, knew he'd seen her. She returned his kiss and felt a surge of satisfaction and pleasure, because she knew his perfect goal would never have been scored if it were not for her.

She heard a voice.

'Now your Jacky's well again. He'll go to the very top of the game. And you'll go with him.'

She looked to her right. Wilf Shadbolt sat next to her, still in the old Greyport colours.

'Look after each other,' he said. *'Goodbye now.'*

Then he faded away, and Alex knew he would never come again.

Leabharlanna Fhine Gall